MW01253623

Blynk & The Magic Slippers

Author: Dorothy L. Lawton

Illustrator: Nataly Vits

DEDICATION

This story was written by Mom when we were young after Jane broke a lamp with figurines on it. It has now been given new life, some fifty years later, by Justin Bates, the only grandchild she was able to hold. And so it is our wish to dedicate this story to you, Justin, for your own dedication to your Nana now. She was, and always will be, so very proud of you.

Her girls, Linda, Jane and Gwen

BLYNK & THE MAGIC SLIPPERS

Gradually Toni's tears subsided, and she smeared her chubby fists across her cheeks, rosy red from the exertion of crying, and left a grimy little furrow to outline the heart that was her face. With a sigh that seemed to carry all the weight of her five-year-old world, she rolled over to her back and, propping her head on folded hands, stared sadly at the dresser lamps.

Usually Toni smiled at Wynk and Blynk, the ceramic pixies that so obligingly held up the pink shades, but tonight she just gazed, emotionless. Then her head toppled sideways with the coming of sleep, and her vision blurred. Her little girl pixie, Blynk, dressed as always in her dainty pink dancing costume, seemed to flutter and sway.......

Suddenly, Toni was dreaming, "Oh, how good it feels," thought Blynk, "when evening comes and that plain old light bulb gives me the energy I need to become alive. What fun to pirouette." And she turned and spun and laughed with joy as she approached her dearest friend, who was Wynk. But in a moment, her face became serious.

"Wynk, What's wrong?" she cried, without a greeting. "Why do you look so unhappy?" Wynk gave his little friend a sad smile. "Oh, Blynk, I'm afraid we may never be able to dance together again nor skip to exciting places. Look at my magic slipper. It's broken. Our little friend Toni wanted to carry me to the kitchen to show me to her Auntie Sue and we had an accident. She felt so badly and her mother was cross, too. I don't know what we can do." Wynk looked so despondent.

Blynk sat down on her satin lamp-stand, hardly knowing what to say. If only Toni had been more careful, or listened to her mother and not touched things at all. For a long time, neither spoke. Then Blynk looked up with an expression that was determined. "Wynk, I must go off alone and find you another pair of magic slippers. You cannot stand in one place forever, can you?

But you must tell me where you think I should look." Blynk arose from her chair to stand in front of her friend.

Wynk did not agree. "You could get lost, Blynk, and it would be so lonely here without you. And think what would happen if you had not returned by morning," he said. "Oh, Wynk," she sighed, "if you do not tell me just where you got the magic slippers for us, then I will surely be lost and not get back."

Wynk looked at his broken shoe before replying, "If you are set on going, dear little Blynk, then listen very carefully. Do you know that your trip might even be dangerous? You know that it is very far! "When she only nodded, he continued, "You and I have often danced up the moon beams to the largest dipper among the stars, so you can get that far. Rest there awhile, and wait for Mrs. Coral, who calls there every hour. Ask her to direct you to the Northern Lights. You have seen them dance often, but they are much farther away than they look. They have magnificent ballet slippers which are made for them by a master craftsman who lives in the northern most country with his little dog, Hanso. It is Hanso who chews the jewel-like leather and puts the magic into the slippers. Sometimes the slippers the master makes are not strong enough for the active Lights, so they are given as rewards to people who deserve them."

"But Wynk," little Blynk was nearly in tears, "how could I ever earn a pair? What could I do?"

"When I went on my adventure. Mrs. Coral told me that anyone who was kind and honest would certainly win the slippers. Do you still want to go?"

"Oh, Wynk, I must go. Indeed I must hurry!" Blynk exclaimed as she tied her bonnet laces more securely. "And please don't worry. I know everything will be fine."

In a moment Blynk was out through the window. For a while she forgot her problems as her feet tapped gently against the light of the moonbeam.

She loved to dance this way, and her magic slippers carried her swiftly-up and up and up! And then she was knocking against the wee flower-shaped door that led to Mrs. Coral's office in the largest dipper among the stars.

She had seen Mrs. Coral only once before. Blynk had been with Wynk, and they had soared farther and farther west. Suddenly they had both realized that they had returned for the third time to the Evening Star- and they were lost. Blynk had been so frightened, although Wynk was brave, telling her they would easily be back to their own lamp stands before dawn, no matter what happened. In no time at all, they had heard a soft voice calling them.

"Little friends, follow me!" Blynk remembered Mrs. Coral's gentle call as she beckoned them, explaining who she was. "It is my quest hour by hour, to be sure that no one becomes lost in our heavens. Let me take you to my home in the largest dipper. It is the easiest place to find among the stars, and anyone who comes can be sure I'll return soon. After you rest a short while and have some star-stem nectar, you'll feel refreshed and able to find your way home!"Mrs. Coral looked a little like a pink fairy with wings as fine as spider webs, and with silvery white hair piled high on her head. And she had the bluest eyes, like the sky when the last cloud has passed-actually shimmering with loveliness. So now, as Blynk waited by Mrs. Coral's door, she knew that it would not be long before she would be guided along her way.

All of a sudden, Blynk heard a tiny noise. At first she thought she must have imagined it, but, as she listened, a soft sound of sobbing seemed to be close by her ear. She peered down the pebbly walk, then through the garden of stardust. And there she was- a wee star fairy, with forlorn-looking brown eyes and tears streaming around her little tipped-up nose. Blynk almost felt sad, too, as she inquired about the trouble.

"Oh! Oh!" the answer was muffled. "I-I- please excuse me, but I just can't stop crying. You see, I just learned that I can't get into music school because I'm too small. The dancing shoes are too heavy, and the musical instruments are just too large. What is to become of a star fairy who can't dance or play? My parents will be disappointed, too, because they wanted us to be family entertainers, Oh, dear, I don't know any star fairies who aren't entertainers."

The little starfairy was quite out of breath when she finished, but she had stopped crying. She stared dolefully at her reflection in the glitter of stardust. Blynk looked at the star fairy's wee feet, and suddenly she knew what would be just the right thing. The yellow lady slippers that grew in the shady nook by the pond near Toni's house were so delicate that even her petite new acquaintance would enjoy wearing them. And-and bluebells grew there, too. She knew that star fairies could make music of all lovely things, and the fragile blue blossoms would be perfect. Excitedly, she described the flowers.

"I will bring you some tomorrow evening," she offered. I would go right now, but I must hurry to the Northern Lights for some magic slippers for my dearest friend."

"Thank you very much." The little star fairy replied, trying to keep her lip from trembling. "You don't even know my name- which is Valerie- and yet you are kind enough to help. But tomorrow night is too late. The great doors of the music school close in five of your hours to prevent any distraction to the learners and- and-."

Blynk interrupted, "Do not worry any more. I can easily get back here by midnight, and it is most probable that I can still complete my second errand after that." She waved a farewell and hurried down the pebbly walk. She did not notice that Mrs. Coral had long before opened the door in response to her knock, and now smiled as she watched her leave.

Blynk was happy to be dancing down the moonbeams again. She sang gaily as she reached the spot where the flowers grew, and picked the two most perfectly-shaped ladyslippers, and the tiniest bluebells she could find. In no time she was dancing again- up and up.

Then before Blynk quite realized what happened, a terrible wind struck her pathway. At first she stumbled on against it; then she fell. An instant later, she cried out as she felt herself being lifted up into the great space above. She could not tell which direction the wind was carrying her, only that she was flying up and down in waves. Her heart hammered in terror as she clutched the flowers against herself, protecting them with both hands. She could scarcely breathe, and her short little body shivered in the cold.

She thought of Wynk. How she wished he were there, she could almost hear him comforting her. "Never, never keep fear in your heart, Blynk. Remember that wasting your energies in feelings of panic and dread keeps you from doing the needful things. And trust that every trouble you over come will bring some good."

"Oh, Wynk!" she tried to control her frantic gasps, "I'll never be as strong as you. I didn't even try to be brave and now I don't know how to get your slippers." Then she had another frightening thought, and she could scarcely keep from sobbing as she whispered , though no one could hear, "What if I don't return to my lamp stand before dawn. Oh, Wynk---

if I should never see you again…" It was almost impossible to believe that anything good could ever come of the storm that still raged about her ears. It tossed her higher and lower in a rocking motion that did make it easier for her to relax, though, and she grew calmer. Wynk would say that a trial had a purpose if only to make one more understanding or more patient or better in some way. But Blynk felt sure that she could never be anything good without Wynk. She would get back to him some way. She clung to that hope, and tried not to think of anything else.

As abruptly as it had begun, the wind stopped. Blynk felt bewildered by the stillness that followed, and she found herself suspended in mid-space, on a cloud of tiny dust particles. In the distance somewhere, she could hear heavenly music, and all the world looked utterly beautiful. The two flowers were still cupped safely in her hand.

Blynk rose and brushed herself off. Immediately she saw the largest dipper among the stars, it seemed so very, very far away. She did not know the hour, but midnight had passed long before. She felt too weary to dance, and too sad, too, because she had failed in her errand for Wynk so completely. Still, if she hurried, she could perhaps reach Mrs. Coral's door in time for wee Valerie to make it to dancing school. No, she could not fail the little starfairy, too!

Blynk trudged on, brushing a tired hand against the wisps of blonde hair which fell against her sand-heavy eyes. Her kerchief had blown off in the wind. After a long , long time she lifted her gaze from the pathway and was dismayed to see that her destination didn't seem much closer. She began to run and even tried to dance, but she lacked the strength. She tripped, but then scrambled up to try to run once more. Again she fell.

As she picked herself up, Blynk knew that someone was beside her even before she looked up to see Mrs. Coral reaching for her hand. "Oh, Mrs. Coral," Blynk cried, " I'm so glad to see you. You are so good to go out looking for all the lost folk. Could you possibly help me to reach your pebbly walk, where…"

Mrs. Coral gave Blynk a quick hug as she interrupted, "I know, my dear. You have the sweetest yellow slippers and a dear wee bell for Valerie, I see. I also see a kind and generous pixie, and a brave one, too. All the heavens will be proud of you. Now-would you like me to take Valerie's new gifts to her for you? Then you could begin your journey back directly."

"Oh, would you, please?" Surprised, Blynk smiled at last. "Thank you ever so much. Then at least I won't lose Wynk. Mrs. Coral, you are the kindest soul."

Mrs. Coral smiled, too, and Blynk wondered how she had managed to keep her silvery hair in perfect order throughout the terrible windstorm. She did not ask, though. "Before you go, then," Mrs. Coral said, still smiling," let me give you some star stem nectar. I knew you'd need some to refresh you enough to dance again."

This time Blynk stammered, "I seem to be saying 'Thank you' over and over. But how could you know that I was anywhere out here?" Too late she realized that Mrs. Coral would think the question bold and rude. But Mrs. Coral only smiled again. "My dear, I heard you talking with Valerie last evening, and I could not leave you on your own, could I now? I watched for you to return, and when the wind carried you away, I hurried as quickly as I could to meet you. That strong breeze is really a friend, Blynk, and while it took you from your path, he was helping another with a more urgent need along the way. And he did not harm you, did he?"

"No, " Blynk answered honestly, "If I had not been so frightened and upset, I'd have enjoyed the ride. And I can always try again tomorrow night to find the magic slippers for Wynk." Blynk sighed with relief as she swallowed the sweet nectar Mrs.

Coral passed her in a miniature silver flask.

Although she felt thirsty, she did not empty it. How odd that seemed. "It's a magic flask, you see," Mrs. Coral explained as she watched Blynk's surprise. "I brought it along just for you, and you may have it. There are rewards, you know, of some kind for generous deeds such as you have done. Not everyone would have troubled themselves to such an extent over Valerie's problems, especially with an important errand of her own."

Then Blynk remembered what her friend had said. But Wynk had received magic slippers instead. How she wished she had deserved the slippers too! Mrs. Coral spoke again. "I know just what you are thinking, my dear, but you will be happy with the silver flask, I think. You noticed that it didn't empty, this time, didn't you? When it is good for you to have some nectar, it will be there. Remember it is magic, and when you need help of other kinds as well, you will know then how this flask can serve you."

How much I have to thank you for, Blynk thought, But before she could speak, Mrs. Coral was already far in the distance, calling, "There are others who will need me now, and it is time for you to be on your way, too."

Blynk blew a kiss after her, then turned to the flask. She was a real Doubting Tom, she then reflected, but how could this be better than the slippers she wanted so much? Then she realized she wasn't exhausted at all anymore. She could skip so high and tap her toes ever so lightly down the moonbeams once again. She had just reached the window, though, when her night time path vanished. Streams of daylight would soon appear.

"Welcome back!" Wynk cried from his lamp stand."I was beginning to believe I should never have agreed to your going. It was a long night without you," he added.

Blynk hurried over to give her friend a hug. "I'm a mess, I know, and I have a flask instead of slippers, but I am so glad to see you again. For awhile I was so afraid---" She broke off with a grin. "I always plunge headlong into everything, don't I?"

As the tidied herself, she recounted her adventures of the night. When she finished, she added with a sigh, "More than anything I wanted those slippers, though. How can I think this flask is a greater reward?"

Wynk spoke thoughtfully," It will serve more purposes, of course, and I may still find slippers somehow, though I will never let you go again, grateful as I am to you for tonight- and proud, too." Just then Blynk's eyes opened wide and she put her fingers to her mouth. "Wynk," she was almost breathless with surprise and excitement.

"Mrs. Coral said that when I needed to know when and how to use this flask, why- then I would know. Now-please hand me your broken slipper."

Just as though she had been told what to do, Blynk opened the flask and poured a silver sticky liquid on the broken parts, then fitted them together. They stuck like magic, as indeed they were. She returned the fixed shoe to Wynk with a flourish. He bowed, his slipper as good as new, although a small white line still showed, and held out his arms to his partner. But they had little time to dance, for Toni was turning in her bed.

Relaxing quietly once more in their comfortable lamp stands, they watched, unstirring, as the five-year-old girl yawned and opened her eyes. Immediately Toni's eyes grew wider. Quickly she hopped out of bed to touch her pixie's foot.

"Thank you, little Blynk," she whispered. " I just wish I could tell Mother, but she would never believe how it happened. Probably she'll say that Grandfather slipped in somehow to fix it so that things can be happy at our house again. But I'm glad I know about magic, even if it is always kept secret from grown-ups.

"Oh, and Blynk, you have tidied up from the night and so must I. The mirror says my face is dirty still." She looked closely at the little girl pixie's hand, and decided, "Yes, I'm sure your fist is cupped differently, and hiding a tiny, tiny flask."

Toni started out of her bedroom door, then turned to add, " Maybe the next time I want to touch forbidden things, you could use some of that magic to keep my feet going straight ahead."

ABOUT THE AUTHOR

Born Dorothy Lois Rauhaula of Ponoka, Alberta. Dorothy was a gifted writer and poet from an early age. June 29, 1957 she married Derrick Lawton, and they set up home in Eckville, Alberta where they had three daughters, Linda, Jane and Gwen.

Dorothy's passion was teaching. She taught high school English and Drama, as well as Sunday school at the Eckville Presbyterian Church. She played the organ, organized many church programs and gatherings and wrote weekly columns of Bible stories for children for many years.

Her greatest joy, however, was when she became "Nana" to Justin, her first grandchild. She laughed that she didn't know anything about baby boys, but soon thereafter declared she should like a "grandchildren farm". She was very devoted to Justin, and would have taken such delight in the eight to come, as well as her several great grandchildren now.

To each of you, we repeat her lecture of being educated and independent. Her life lessons would be "Do what you love wherever and however you need to do it, and regardless of the expectations of others", "Be generous with your time" , "Defend and protect those you love" and "Have faith in God".

Dorothy L Lawton
August 29,1933-August 22,1979

Dorothy L. Lawton

20103428R00015

Made in the USA
San Bernardino, CA
28 December 2018